I celebrated World Book Day 2022
with this gift from my local
bookseller, Joanna Nadin,
Rikin Parekh and Bloomsbury.
#ShareAStory

WORLD BOOK DAY

WORLD BOOK DAY'S mission is to offer every child and young person the opportunity to read and love books by giving you the chance to have a book of your own.

To find out more, and for fun activities, including our monthly book club, video stories and book recommendations, visit **worldbookday.com**

WORLD BOOK DAY is a charity funded by publishers and booksellers in the UK and Ireland.

WORLD BOOK DAY is also made possible by generous sponsorship from National Book Tokens and support from authors and illustrators.

Mrs Bottomley-Blunt

Headmistress.
Has a long, laminated List of Rules.
Makes a noise like a horse when
she is annoyed, which is a lot.

Mr Nidgett

Teacher of 4B.
Firm believer that
everything can be
mended with kindn
Often proved wror

Stanley Bradshaw

Fond of footling, fiddle-faddling
and shilly-shallying, much to
Mrs Bottomley-Blunt's annoyance.

Manjit Morris

Stanley's best friend.
Determined to be the First Human
Boy ever to do a lot of dangerous,
foolish and impossible things.

Keith Mears

Self-proclaimed King of the Internet.
Falls asleep in class a lot.

PRIMARY

Lionel Dawes

Called Lionel, even though she is a girl, because her mum says names do not have genders, they are just words, which is true if you think about it, but Mrs Bottomley-Blunt does not agree.

Bruce Bingley

Once got a plastic brontosaurus stuck up his nose for a week. Can burp the national anthem.

Lacey Braithwaite

Compulsive liar.

Penelope Potts

Muriel Lemon

Knows too many medical facts. Fond of warning Mr Nidgett of the dangers of everything.

Annoying telltale. Identical twin of Hermione Potts in 4A, and determined to join her by fair means or foul.

Harvey Barlow

Eater of many biscuits. Often mistaken for a Year 6.

Books by Joanna Nadin

The Worst Class in the World

The Worst Class in the World
Gets Worse

The Worst Class in the World
Dares You!

The Worst Class in the World
in Danger! (World Book Day)

Joanna Nadin

THE
WORST
CLASS
IN THE
WORLD
IN DANGER!

Illustrated by Rikin Parekh

BLOOMSBURY
CHILDREN'S BOOKS
LONDON   OXFORD   NEW YORK   NEW DELHI   SYDNEY

BLOOMSBURY CHILDREN'S BOOKS
Bloomsbury Publishing Plc
50 Bedford Square, London WC1B 3DP, UK
29 Earlsfort Terrace, Dublin 2, Ireland

BLOOMSBURY, BLOOMSBURY CHILDREN'S BOOKS and the Diana logo
are trademarks of Bloomsbury Publishing Plc

First published in Great Britain in 2022 by Bloomsbury Publishing Plc

A catalogue record for this book is available from the British Library

ISBN: PB: 978-1-5266-4273-8

2 4 6 8 10 9 7 5 3 1

Printed and bound in Great Britain by CPI Group (UK) Ltd,
Croydon CR0 4YY

To find out more about our authors and books visit
www.bloomsbury.com
and sign up for our newsletters

To Felix and Hamish

— J.N.

For Park Lane Primary School and
Barham Primary School — where I learned how
to draw and fell in love with books!

— R.P.

Our class is the **WORST CLASS IN THE WORLD**.

I know it is the **WORST CLASS IN THE WORLD** because Mrs Bottomley-Blunt (who is our headmistress, and who makes a noise like a horse when she is annoyed, which is a lot) is always taking our teacher into the corridor and saying,

'Mr Nidgett, I have come across some rotten eggs in my time, but 4B is **LITERALLY** the **WORST CLASS IN THE WORLD**.'

LITERALLY means actually scientifically **TRUE**. Mrs Bottomley-Blunt pointed that out when Manjit Morris (who is my best friend, and who is going to be the First Human Boy to Tunnel to the Centre of the Earth) said his head had **LITERALLY** exploded when he got a dog called Killer for his birthday, and it actually hadn't.

It is true that a lot of things do not go as well as they could in class 4B. For example:

1. The time Manjit swapped Killer for Bradley Hunt's (who is First Toughest in Year 6) key ring with a one-eyed monkey on it and Killer did a poo in Bradley's mum's airing cupboard.

2. The time Harvey Barlow made a volcano with thirteen minty sweets and some fizzy pop and it caused a foam explosion.

3. The time we went on a class trip to an art gallery and Keith Mears did

some modern art with a sandwich and a priceless artefact and now we are banned from the gallery for life.

Plus no one has won a prize all year, and 4A have won:

1. Best Mural about Penguins

2. Best Gymnastic Display without Any Injuries

3. Best Being Quiet in Assembly without Even Making Sniffing Sounds

Although this is not surprising, as their class captain is Eustace Troy,

who is president of chess club,
first violin in the school orchestra
and team leader on the Shining
Examples competitive spelling
squad.

Our class captain is Bruce
Bingley, who can only burp the
national anthem, which I think

is quite impressive, but Mrs
Bottomley-Blunt does not.

She says school is not about
footling or fiddle-faddling or **FUN**.
It is about **LEARNING** and it is high
time we tried harder to **EXCEL** at it.

Dad says well at least I haven't
been arrested. Grandpa says being
arrested would be getting off lightly
and **IN HIS DAY** he had to walk
five miles to school barefoot and
eat gravel for lunch.

Mum, who works at the council,
says, 'I have spent all day listening

to Mr Butterworth bang on about lamp posts and the last thing I need is a heated debate about eating gravel. As long as Stanley's happy, that's all that matters.'

And you know what? I am happy, because:

1. According to Mr Nidgett, everyone excels at something, even Harvey Barlow – they just have to look very hard to find it.

2. According to the laws of probability, we have had all our bad luck and nothing else can possibly go wrong.

3. According to Manjit, even if it does go wrong we have a FOOLPROOF PLAN to get away with it, which is DO NOT TELL ANYONE.

You see, 4B may be the **WORST CLASS IN THE WORLD**. But I like it.

Harvey Barlow says it's Manjit's fault for supergluing a sausage to my head so I could wrestle a cat and be like Mavis Grady, Danger Lady.

Manjit says it's Harvey Barlow's

fault for trying to eat the sausage so he could be sick and be like Mavis Grady, Danger Lady.

Muriel Lemon says it's Mrs Bottomley-Blunt's fault for inviting Mavis Grady, Danger Lady into school in the first place when everyone knows danger isn't something to be **MESSED WITH**.

Mr Nidgett says he doesn't actually care whose fault it is, as long as the **DANGER**

MADNESS is finished or he will **LITERALLY** resign from teaching and knit himself an igloo because it cannot be harder than this.

I don't know whose fault it is, but I do know it started on Tuesday.

What happened was we were in history arguing about who would win in a fight: Henry VIII or Manjit with a superpowered laser destructor gun, and Manjit was just about to demonstrate how on Harvey Barlow with a plastic ruler

(because he hasn't invented the superpowered laser destructor gun yet) when Mrs Bottomley-Blunt walked in and said, 'How many times, Manjit Morris? Rulers are for drawing lines, not for fighting. That is against the rules, as well you know, so that is minus two stars and the Disappointing Day board for you.'

And Mr Nidgett was about to explain that the ruler was being used in the interests of history when Mrs Bottomley-Blunt said,

'And another thing. What on earth are you all doing in here **FOOTLING** around when it is time to meet our Special Guest and you should be in the hall sitting in a row and not saying even one word? Chop-chop!'

And none of us had anything to say to that, not even Penelope Potts (who always has something to say, and it is usually that it is not fair she is in 4B when her twin

17

sister, Hermione, is in 4A) OR Mr Nidgett, and so we chop-chopped to the hall with everyone else at St Regina's Primary and sat in a row and only said seventeen words, which Mr Nidgett said was at least

an improvement on last week.

And Manjit said, 'Now it's twenty-five words.'

And Bruce Bingley said, 'Now it's thirty words!'

And Manjit was about to say

it was thirty-four words when Mr Nidgett said it was a shame we didn't manage maths like that in class but could we please be quiet before Mrs Bottomley-Blunt put **HIM** on the Disappointing Day board.

But before Mrs Bottomley-Blunt could even think about doing this, something **LITERALLY** incredible happened, which was that there was a *whoosh-whoosh* sound outside and everyone rushed to the big windows to see what it was

and it was a helicopter about to

land on the grass. And everyone

went, 'Ooooh,' except for Manjit,

who whispered that whoever was

in the helicopter would regret

landing there because Mr Spigot

(who is our caretaker, and who has

one ear bigger than the other) had
only just mown it, and also now
it was about fifty words. Which is
when Mrs Bottomley-Blunt told us
all to SIT DOWN because we were
breaking about twenty-seven rules,
and to wait quietly for our Special
Guest.

And we did all sit down, but we
did not wait quietly, because we
were too busy guessing who the
Special Guest might be.

Manjit said it would probably
be the PRIME MINISTER.

Keith Mears said it would
probably be the **QUEEN**.

Bruce Bingley said it would
probably be his **MUM**, who is the
OVERLORD OF THE UNIVERSE, and
so is better than the Queen and the
Prime Minister put together.

And I was just about to point
out that last week Bruce said his

mum **WAS** the Prime Minister,

when everyone went **MAD** with

excitement because the Special

Guest appeared in the hall and it

wasn't the Prime Minister or the

Queen or Bruce Bingley's mum,

it was Mavis Grady, Danger Lady,

who is very famous for doing lots

of **DANGEROUS** and **ADVENTUROUS**

things and writing about them in

a book called an autobiography,

which means everything in it is

LITERALLY true. And she was

definitely **EXTREMELY** special,

because she was wearing the sort of shorts explorers wear, and a massive hat, and a necklace made of shark's teeth. And she told us all about the **DANGEROUS** and **AMAZING** things she had done, e.g.:

1. The time she wrestled an alligator in the swamps of Florida and WON.

2. The time she was attacked by a black mamba (which is a deadly snake) in the desert in Africa and wrestled that as well and WON.

3. The time she climbed the tallest tree in a rainforest to save a monkey with a sore arm from a jaguar, which she also wrestled and WON.

But the most **AMAZING** thing of all was that once upon a time she was a pupil at St Regina's Primary, i.e. **OUR** school, so in fact it proved that **ANYONE** could become rich and famous, especially if you did **DANGEROUS** and **ADVENTUROUS** things. Which Manjit said he was definitely going to do from now on, only Mrs Bottomley-Blunt said no he wouldn't, he would do something safe and useful like learning his times tables, and did anyone have any questions.

And everyone stuck their hand up really high and went, 'Me, me.'

Mrs Bottomley-Blunt said, '**SENSIBLE** questions!'

So most of us put our hands

down, except Eustace Troy, who said, 'Why was the black mamba in the desert when everyone knows they live in forests?'

Mavis Grady said because it was an especially **DANGEROUS** and **ADVENTUROUS** black mamba, which was exciting and we all said so.

Then Muriel Lemon (whose parents are both doctors, and who is excused from all dangerous activities, e.g. netball, football and science experiments), said, 'Everything you've done is against **HEALTH AND SAFETY** advice and common sense and it is amazing you are not dead yet,' which Mavis Grady said wasn't actually a question, so didn't require an answer (which is true if you think about it).

Penelope Potts then said, 'Were you in class 4A or 4B?' And Mavis Grady said she was in 4A, which was disappointing and we all said so. Only 4A were **PLEASED AS PUNCH**, which means very pleased indeed.

And that was the end of the talk except for Mrs Bottomley-Blunt saying that we could read more about all the **DANGEROUS** and **ADVENTUROUS** things in Mavis Grady's autobiography book, which only cost £9.99.

Only none of us had £9.99, because none of us had remembered to take the letter

home and get money from our
parents, not even Penelope Potts.

Harvey Barlow only had half

 a jammy

biscuit

and a pencil

sharpener.

Lacey Braithwaite only had
a hair clip in the shape of a
strawberry and some crisp dust.

Manjit only had four raisins
and a dirty coin that he found
behind the Poo Wagon (which is
not actually a wagon made of poo,

it is the temporary boys' toilets, because Manjit broke the real ones, but that's another story) that almost **DEFINITELY** belonged to the Romans.

Only Mr Nidgett said it did not, it was just a worn-out 2p. But that it didn't matter, because **HE** had £9.99 and **HE** would buy a book and **HE** would read it to us if we didn't get up to any **HOO-HA** on our way back to the classroom. And amazingly we only got up to a little bit, i.e. arguing over who would win in a fight, Henry VIII or Mavis Grady, Danger Lady (and it was Mavis Grady), which Mr Nidgett said did not count, so he would still read to us. Which he did.

Only when he had finished reading about the time Mavis Grady got trapped in an underwater cave with a shark and had to wrestle it and **WON**, Mr Nidgett said he had had an idea, which was that we would all write our own autobiography for homework tonight and whoever wrote the most **INTERESTING** one would **WIN** the copy of Mavis Grady, Danger Lady's book. But that the winning autobiography had to be completely **TRUE**.

And almost immediately everyone was **MAD** with excitement about what they would write about.

Keith Mears said he would write about the day he wrestled a very angry puma and WON.

Bruce Bingley said he would write about the day he wrestled a very angry puma AND a swarm of endangered wasps and WON.

Manjit said he would write about the day he became the First Human Boy to Wrestle a Very Angry Puma, a Swarm of Endangered Wasps and the Overlord of the Universe and WON.

Mr Nidgett said unless we had

LITERALLY wrestled anything then could we not write about that.

So Lionel Dawes (who is called Lionel even though she is a girl, because her mum says names do not have genders, they are just words, which is true if you think about it) said could she write about the day she asked her own cat, Dave (who is called Dave even though it is a girl), to not eat a mouse because she does not believe in eating

38

anything with a face or wrestling,
only she did not **WIN**. And Mr
Nidgett said yes she could.

Only Manjit said that story
wasn't **INTERESTING**, so she would
definitely not win the copy of
Mavis Grady, Danger Lady's book.

And Lionel said, 'Is.'

And Manjit said, 'Isn't.'

And Lionel said, 'Is.'

And Manjit said, 'Isn't.'

But Mr Nidgett said he would be
the judge of what was interesting
and what was not tomorrow

morning, and in the meantime could we please get on with trying to use a semicolon in a sentence and we did and not one of us got it right, not even Penelope Potts.

But I didn't care, because Manjit said he had a **FOOLPROOF PLAN** and to meet him behind the Poo Wagon at lunch so I did.

At the Poo Wagon, Manjit explained his **DANGEROUS** and **ADVENTUROUS** plan, and it was that we would **FIND** a wild animal in the playground, persuade it to wrestle us, and then we would write about it and it would be absolutely true and so WE would win the book about Mavis Grady, Danger Lady.

I said there were not many wild animals lurking in the playground, unless you counted the Ghost Pigeon, some ants, and some newts, but we weren't allowed near the pond after the time Keith Mears swallowed Newt Pond Water for a dare and claimed it had given him special newt superpowers but it hadn't.

Only Harvey Barlow, who was also behind the Poo Wagon eating biscuits, which is against Mrs Bottomley-Blunt's rules, said ants weren't dangerous.

Muriel Lemon, who was also behind the Poo Wagon (because everyone else was doing skipping and she isn't allowed)

said actually ants were very dangerous and a man called Julian Hooley had once died after being bitten by a million of them, only they were special poisonous ones.

Harvey Barlow said our ants did not look like special poisonous ones, they looked like normal ants. But Manjit, who was quite angry by then, said we would not be wrestling ants, because he had a better plan and we would do it after school and it was **FOOLPROOF** so to **SHUT UP** about ants.

Manjit's new plan was this: We would find a wild animal on the way home, wrestle it, and then when we got back to Manjit's house we would write all about it. And I agreed that this plan was definitely **FOOLPROOF**.

But on the way home the only wild animals we saw were:

1. Mr Spigot's dog, Fester, who is about a hundred in dog years, and who did not seem keen to wrestle

us because he was eating one of Mr Nidgett's Emergency Shoes.

2. A pigeon (only a normal one, not the ghost one from the Smelly Death Log, who everyone says will eat you if you even touch the log for more than a second), who did not seem keen to wrestle us because it was eating some crisp dust.

3. Lionel's cat, Dave, who did not seem keen to wrestle us as she was eating a dead squirrel, which we decided not to tell Lionel about because of the face thing.

By the time we got back to
Manjit's house, he was full of
GLOOM because of not being
able to do the most **DANGEROUS**
and **ADVENTUROUS** thing so we
would not win the Mavis Grady,
Danger Lady book. I said perhaps
we could wrestle Killer, who is
Manjit's dog, and Manjit said that
was a **FOOLPROOF** idea and we
went straight to the back garden.
Only when we got there Killer
did not seem keen to wrestle us
either because she was too busy

barking at next door's cat, Lollipop, who was at the top of the apple tree and was refusing to come down.

And that is when I had my **BRILLIANT** idea, which was that we could **RESCUE** Lollipop from the top of the tree, which was **DANGEROUS** and **ADVENTUROUS**, and then we could write about that. And Manjit said yes and that once we had rescued her, we could also **WRESTLE** Lollipop and in fact it was **FOOLPROOF** and so he wasn't full of **GLOOM** any more.

Manjit's house is **OUTSTANDING**, because he is allowed to do all sorts of things that I am not. For example:

1. Try to be the First Human Boy to Dangle Off the Living-Room Door for an Hour.
2. Try to be the First Human Boy to Invent Gold.
3. Use the ladder in the garage to get halfway up the apple

tree so that Lollipop can jump into
the rescuer's arms, when I am not
even allowed to LOOK at our tree, not
after last time.

Then Manjit
said it should be
me going up the
tree because he
was going to do
the wrestling,
and that was

FAIR, and I am keen on being **FAIR**,
so I did.

Only when I got up there,
Lollipop did not seem at all excited
to jump into my arms, and in
fact moved even further along

the top branch. But Manjit wasn't **DETERRED**, which means put off. He said what we needed was something to **LURE** her down, e.g. a sausage, and luckily there was one in the fridge and Mr Morris hadn't eaten it yet, so we could use it, and so we did.

So I climbed down the ladder to get the sausage, and then started to climb back up the ladder with the sausage in one hand, only it turns out it is quite hard to climb up a ladder with a sausage in one hand

But Manjit wasn't **DETERRED**. He said in fact what we needed was to **GLUE** the sausage to my head so my hands would be free for climbing and luckily there was some glue in the cupboard, and he was allowed to use it, and so he did.

Then once the sausage was **GLUED** to my head, I climbed all the way back up the ladder and up the tree as well on to the very top branch where Lollipop was.

Only that is when it all went **WRONG**.

Because once I had got up the tree, Lollipop decided she did not need rescuing after all, and hopped off the tree on to next door's garage roof. Only **I DID** need rescuing because I had gone too far up the tree and the ladder wasn't tall enough to reach me and Mr Morris doesn't climb trees because of being an **UNDISCOVERED GENIUS**, so we had to call Mrs Morris, who is a police officer, and she had to call the fire brigade to bring a special extendable ladder to get me down.

Then worst of all, the glue was **SUPERGLUE**, which means it does not come off, not **EVER**, and so there was still a lot of sausage stuck to my head, even after we persuaded Killer to eat most of it.

So Manjit was full of **GLOOM** again because we hadn't managed to wrestle anything and so we would not win the Mavis Grady, Danger Lady book, and I was full of **GLOOM** because I would be in trouble with my mum because of the sausage.

Only Mrs Morris said why
didn't we write the story of getting
stuck up a tree, because that
was definitely **DANGEROUS** and
ADVENTUROUS as well as being
TRUE, and also she would ring
my mum and say I was having
a sleepover because the sausage
would probably be gone by the
time I got home tomorrow. And
me and Manjit agreed that,
even though we hadn't wrestled
anything, this plan was definitely
FOOLPROOF because there was

no way anyone else in 4B would have got stuck up a tree **AND** been rescued by the fire brigade **AND** have sausage stuck on their head **AND** so we would win the Mavis Grady, Danger Lady book after all.

So we did write it. And the most **AMAZING** thing of all was that it was even more fun than doing the **DANGEROUS** thing in the first place, because we could eat biscuits while we did it and not even nearly fall out of a tree.

When we got to school the next morning everyone was **MAD** with excitement to read their **TRUE** stories out.

Keith Mears read out the story of the time he tried to swap his brother for a packet of crisps (which is true).

Harvey Barlow read out the story of the time he ate too many biscuits and was sick on Mr Nidgett's shoes (which is true).

Bruce Bingley read out the story of the time he ate a fly and absorbed the fly's superpowers and was sick on anyone who crossed him and the sick was Supersick and melted them into infinity (which was not true and Manjit said so).

Only Bruce said, 'Is, and anyway your story about the cat and the fire brigade and the sausage isn't true!'

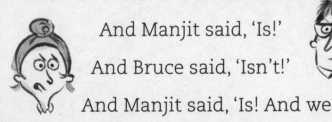

And Manjit said, 'Is!'

And Bruce said, 'Isn't!'

And Manjit said, 'Is! And we

have the sausage to prove it.'

So Bruce said in that case he would **WRESTLE** Manjit to prove his story was the best and so he would win the book.

Then Harvey Barlow said in fact he would eat the rest of the sausage and be sick on Mr Nidgett's shoes again and so **HE** would win the book.

And Muriel Lemon said she would go to Mrs Pickens (who is our school secretary and who smells of soup) and get her to call Dr and Dr Lemon, who would report everyone for **DANGEROUS** activity and the school would probably be closed for **HEALTH AND SAFETY** reasons and then we would all be sorry.

And we were all shouting that we would not be sorry **AT ALL**

when Mrs Bottomley-Blunt walked in.

She said, 'Bruce Bingley, why are you holding Manjit Morris upside down by the ankles and, Harvey Barlow, why are you eating Stanley Bradshaw's hair? These are

against the rules, as well you know. Minus four house points and the Disappointing Day board for all of you. Honestly, Mr Nidgett, I have come across some rotten eggs in my time, but 4B is **LITERALLY** the **WORST CLASS IN THE WORLD.**'

Then she stomped off out again.

Which is when Mr Nidgett said he

didn't actually care whose fault

it was, as long as the **DANGER**

MADNESS was finished, or he

would **LITERALLY** resign from

teaching and knit himself an igloo

because it cannot be harder than

this.

When I got home, Grandpa

said, 'Why have you got bits of

sausage stuck to your head?

Was the Special Guest one of

those Celebrity Chefs?'

I said no, and it was a long story, but a true one, and it was all because we wanted to have a **DANGEROUS** adventure that could go in a book.

Dad said, 'I could have been an adventurer, but my knees are a bit tricksy.'

Grandpa said, '**IN MY DAY** we couldn't afford adventure, we made do with spinning in a circle until we were **SICK**.'

Mum said, 'I've just spent all

day listening to Mr Butterworth
bang on about brick walls and the
last thing I need is a heated debate
about sick. As long as Stanley's
happy, that's all that matters.'

And you know what? I am.
Because Muriel Lemon won
the Mavis Grady, Danger Lady
autobiography with her story

about the time she
did not wrestle
anything because
of the **DANGER**, but
it meant she read

a really **INTERESTING** book about bees instead.

And it turns out that Mavis Grady, Danger Lady had **MADE UP** a lot of the things she had wrestled and **WON** so her book wasn't an autobiography, it was just another story after all.

And so 4A isn't **PLEASED AS PUNCH** any more, but 4B is. Because it all goes to show we don't even have to do **DANGEROUS** things to be famous, we could just write about them instead.

Could
you be in

THE

WORST

CLASS

IN THE

WORLD?

Turn over and take
a fun quiz to find out!

1. Have you ever used a plastic ruler as a pretend superpowered laser destructor gun?
YES or NO

2. Have you ever done something DANGEROUS and ADVENTUROUS?
YES or NO

3. Have you ever persuaded a wild animal to wrestle with you?
YES or NO

4. Have you ever climbed a ladder to rescue a cat from a tree?
YES or NO

5. Have you ever tried to lure a cat down from a tree with a sausage superglued to your head?
YES or NO

6. Have you ever got stuck in a tree and needed the fire brigade to get you down?
YES or NO

Read more hilarious HIGH JINKS with
THE WORST CLASS IN THE WORLD

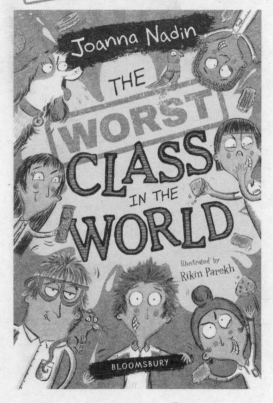

Find out what happens when Stanley and Manjit have a FOOLPROOF PLAN to become the Biscuit Kings of 4B and to win Show and Tell ...

WARNING: Contains soggy shoes, a hamster skeleton and loads of sick!

Read more hilarious HIGH JINKS with
THE WORST CLASS IN THE WORLD

Guess what happens when Stanley and Manjit want
to become the best playground monitors EVER and
when they rescue a penguin from the zoo ...

**WARNING: Contains flooding toilets,
fish-finger-and-pickle sandwiches
and penguin poop!**

Read more hilarious HIGH JINKS with
THE WORST CLASS IN THE WORLD

You won't believe what happens when 4B tries to
catch NITS and to beat each other at DARES!

WARNING: Contains flying minibeasts,
pooey pond water and really stinky burps!

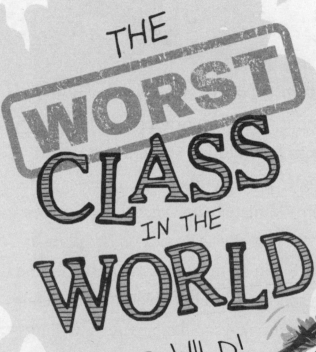

AND LOOK OUT FOR MORE
HILARIOUS HIGH JINKS WHEN

THE
WORST
CLASS
IN THE
WORLD

GOES WILD!

COMING SOON!

Joanna Nadin is an award-winning author who has written more than eighty books for children. She has also been a juggler, a lifeguard and an adviser to the Prime Minister. The worst thing she ever did at school was be sick on her plate at lunch and blame it on someone else. She lives in Bath and her favourite things are goats, monkeys and crisps. As a lifelong lover of books, she is LITERALLY over the moon (in Manjit's terms) to support World Book Day.

Rikin Parekh (aka Mr Rik) is an author/illustrator and ninja. He also works in primary school as an LSA. The worst thing he ever did at school was to draw all over his exercise books! He lives in Wembley and his favourite things are pizza, dogs, and picking his nose and collecting the bogeys. Books have opened many wonderful doors for Rikin, so EVERY DAY feels like World Book Day and he is LITERALLY SO EXCITED to be supporting it!

If you like

THE WORST CLASS IN THE WORLD, check out the

SPACE DETECTIVES

Turn over for a sneak peek!

Chapter 1

Welcome to Starville

It was another perfect day on Starville – the most astonishing place in the galaxy. A gigantic space station, Starville sailed silently overhead in orbit around the Earth and was home to over a million humans and aliens. It was a single, vast city brimming with skyscrapers, lush green parks and even a sparkling artificial sea, all enclosed by a huge and incredibly strong glass dome. Seen through a telescope from the world below, it looked like a gleaming snow globe gliding majestically through the night sky.

At the edge of a wide, tree-lined square near the centre of Starville's fanciest shopping district, two ten-year-old human boys stood behind an ice cream stall. One was tall, gawky and looked a bit like an ostrich wearing glasses. His name was Connor. The other was short, squat and constantly bristling with energy like a terrier. This was Ethan.

The square was full of humans and aliens enjoying the sunshine. Business at the ice cream stall was brisk.

'Wow,' said Ethan as he watched their latest customers, a family of tall, two-legged, blue-skinned, cow-like creatures, walk away licking their lips. 'Those Neptunian Cow People really love our Extra Minty Grapefruit and Smoky Bacon flavour! That's the fifth lot we've sold to them today.'

Connor adjusted his glasses, a sure sign there was something on his mind. 'Actually, Ethan, the Cow People are from *Pluto*, not Neptune. You should try to remember that. We wouldn't want to offend any of our customers.'

Ethan had to laugh. 'Give me a chance, mate! We've only been on Starville a week. I haven't learned all the alien races who live here yet.'

'Well, you could have memorised them all on the rocket trip up here, like I did,' said Connor. 'What were you doing?'

Ethan shrugged. 'Looking out of the

window and going, **"Blimey, I'm on a flipping rocket!"**

That and eating the cakes my mum baked for the trip. You can't learn everything in books, you know. Sometimes you need to just look around you. Or taste around you.' He scooped a stray blob of ice cream from the machine's dispenser nozzle with the end of his finger and popped it in his mouth.

Connor glared at him. 'For the last time, stop doing that. It's unhygienic. You'll get us closed down.'

'Oh yeah,' said Ethan. 'Sorry.'

'Anyway, I'd recommend getting to know all the different alien races now we're here,' said Connor. 'It might be handy for a case.'

'A case!' said Ethan, staring off into the distance. 'That's what we need!'

'Tell me about it,' grumbled Connor, folding his arms. 'I hardly think standing around all day selling ice cream is a good use of our skills.'

These boys were more than just ice cream sellers. They were **detectives**! Back home on Earth, Connor and Ethan had solved many mysteries together in their spare time, such as finding their head teacher's missing antique letter opener (long story short: magpie). As a result, the two boys had got rather good at finding the solutions to people's thorny problems. So when Ethan's Uncle Nick had invited them to spend the long summer holidays working on his ice cream stall on Starville, the pair had accepted instantly. This was their chance to be *Space Detectives*!

The only problem was that, so far, there didn't seem to be any mysteries on Starville to solve. Neither the impressive Space Detectives website they had created nor the adverts they posted online had brought them a single case. Well, that wasn't quite true. There had been the Case of the Stolen Priceless Fob Watch. But unfortunately this had turned very quickly into the Case of the Priceless Fob Watch That Someone Thought Was Stolen But Which Turned Out After Only Five Minutes of Looking Simply to Be in the Pocket of Their Other

Waistcoat, so there wasn't really much of a mystery to solve there. Was there no one aboard this space station who needed their help?

'One scoop of Triple Choc in a sugar-frosted waffle cone, please!' said a bright voice.

Roused from their daydream, the boys found they had a new customer. She was a human girl of about their age with two short pigtails, a T-shirt with an animated image of a cat on it, and a very expensive-looking striped bag slung over one shoulder.

'Sure thing,' said Ethan, and pressed the button on the ice cream machine labelled Triple Choc.

Ffffffzzzzssssssplatttttt!

A jet of liquid ice cream sprayed from its nozzle straight into Ethan's face.

Bleeugh!!!

'Connor? Something's up with this thing! Uncle Nick will go barmy if we've broken his ice cream machine.'

Connor rolled his eyes at their customer. 'Excuse my friend. He isn't the most technical person in the world.' He swiftly examined a small touchscreen on the ice cream machine, adjusted a setting and pressed the button.

Fffffffzzzzsssssssplattttttt!

He too received a jet of liquid ice cream in the face.

Connor removed his glasses and wiped the lenses on his shirt. 'Ah. Obviously some kind of malfunction.'

'Excuse my friend,' said Ethan. 'Turns out he isn't the most technical person in the world either.' He winked at Connor, who gave him a sheepish grin.

The girl leaned over the counter to

examine the touchscreen. 'Do you mind? I know a little about computers.'

'Be our guest,' said Ethan, waggling his head to dislodge ice cream from his ears.

Swiftly, the girl's fingers danced over the touchscreen. 'Ah, *of course*,' she said. 'Your ice cream machine has the Misty 54 virus. It's a new one. Quite nasty.'

'A virus?' asked Ethan. 'So that's why it sprayed that stuff all over us? It sneezed?'

Connor shook his head. 'She means a *computer* virus. A rogue computer program that gets into people's devices and stops them working properly.'

'Fortunately for you,' said the girl, 'programming is my hobby and I'm a bit of an expert when it comes to computer viruses.' Once again her fingers tripped lightly over the touchscreen. There was a pleasing electronic jingle and a message appeared saying, **Misty 54 virus erased. All systems working normally.** 'Try it now.'

Ethan pushed the Triple Choc button again and the machine dispensed one perfect scoop of Triple Choc ice cream in a sugar-frosted waffle cone. He handed it to the girl. 'Here you go! No charge!'

'My pleasure,' said the girl, and, with a friendly wave, she sauntered away.

Connor nudged Ethan in the ribs. 'How

are we supposed to make any money if you're just going to give the ice cream away?'

'You may be a genius in lots of ways,' said Ethan, 'but trust me when it comes to understanding people. A free ice cream is a *nice* way to thank her for fixing our machine. And she's probably going to tell all her friends how great we are, and then they'll flock here and buy bucketloads of ice cream.'

Connor adjusted his glasses. 'Hmmm. We'll see.'

Suddenly, an ear-splitting roar filled the air, followed by a terrified scream.

'What the heck was that?' asked Connor, startled.

Ethan gasped and pointed at something over Connor's shoulder. 'That, mate,' he said, 'is the sound of someone calling for the Space Detectives. Come on!'

Happy
World Book Day!

Our mission is to encourage every child and young person to enjoy reading, and to have a book of their own.

Everyone is a reader — that includes you!

Whether you enjoy **comics**, **fact books**, **adventure stories**, **recipes** – books are for everyone and every book counts.

On **World Book Day**, everyone comes together to have **FUN** reading. Talking about and sharing books with your friends and family makes reading even more memorable and magic.

WORLD BOOK DAY
3 MARCH 2022

Where will reading journey take you next?

1 Take a trip to your local bookshop

Brimming with brilliant books and helpful booksellers to share awesome reading recommendations, bookshops are magical places. You can even enjoy booky events and meet your favourite authors and illustrators!

Find your nearest bookseller at booksaremybag.com/Home

2 Join your local library

A world awaits your local library, place where all the books you could ever want to read awaits. Even better, you can borrow them for **FREE**! Libraries can offer expert advice on what to read next, as well as free family reading events.

Find your local library at gov.uk/local-library-services

Scan here to visit our website!

3 Check out the World Book Day website

Looking for reading tips, advice and inspiration? There is so much to discover at worldbookday.com/getreading, packed with book recommendations, fun activities, audiobooks, and videos to enjoy on your own or as a family, as well as competitions and all the latest book news galore.

World Book Day* is a charity sponsored by National Book Tokens

NATIONAL BOOK tokens